Dear Parent:
Your child's love of reading

Every child learns to read in a different way and at his or her own speed. Some go back and forth between reading levels and read favorite books again and again. Others read through each level in order. You can help your young reader improve and become more confident by encouraging his or her own interests and abilities. From books your child reads with you to the first books he or she reads alone, there are I Can Read Books for every stage of reading:

SHARED READING
Basic language, word repetition, and whimsical illustrations, ideal for sharing with your emergent reader

BEGINNING READING
Short sentences, familiar words, and simple concepts for children eager to read on their own

READING WITH HELP
Engaging stories, longer sentences, and language play for developing readers

READING ALONE
Complex plots, challenging vocabulary, and high-interest topics for the independent reader

ADVANCED READING
Short paragraphs, chapters, and exciting themes for the perfect bridge to chapter books

I Can Read Books have introduced children to the joy of reading since 1957. Featuring award-winning authors and illustrators and a fabulous cast of beloved characters, I Can Read Books set the standard for beginning readers.

A lifetime of discovery begins with the magical words **"I Can Read!"**

Visit www.icanread.com for information
on enriching your child's reading experience.

ICE AGE™
DAWN OF THE DINOSAURS

Ice Age: Dawn of the Dinosaurs: Momma Mix-Up

Library of Congress Catalog card number: 2009923993
ISBN 978-0-06-168978-9

Typography by Rick Farley

09 10 11 12 13   LP/WOR   10 9 8 7 6 5 4 3 2 1

❖

First Edition

ICE AGE™
DAWN OF THE DINOSAURS

MOMMA MIX-UP

Adapted by Sierra Harimann

HarperCollins*Publishers*

Sid was a sloth.

He lived during the Ice Age.

Sid's friends Ellie and Manny
were having a baby.
Sid was happy for them,
but he felt left out.

Sid looked at himself in the ice.
"At least I still have
my good looks," he said to himself.

CRACK!

The ice broke!

Sid fell and landed in a cave.

It was a strange new place.

There was no ice on the ground.

Sid didn't know where he was.

He saw three large eggs.

"Hello?" he said.

No one answered.

The eggs were all alone.

"Don't worry,"
Sid told the eggs.
"You're not alone anymore.
I'll take care of you!"

Sid tried to roll the eggs home.

But one egg got away.

Oh, no!

The egg rolled off a cliff.

Ellie caught the egg with her trunk.

"Thank you!" Sid said.

"I'm so sorry," he told the egg.

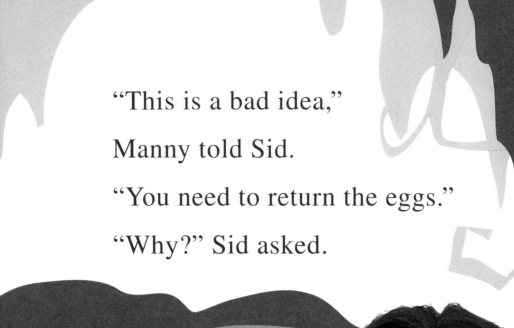

"This is a bad idea,"
Manny told Sid.
"You need to return the eggs."
"Why?" Sid asked.

"Their mother must miss them,"
Ellie told him.

"There was no mother," Sid said.

"We don't know that," Manny said.

"You should return them."

But Sid loved the eggs.

He wanted to keep them.

So he put the eggs on a sled.

Then he pushed the eggs to his cave.

The next day, the eggs hatched.

They were dinosaurs!

The dinosaurs were already very big.

They had sharp teeth.

The dinosaurs saw Sid.

"Momma!" they said.

"I'm a mom!" Sid said proudly.

But the next day,

the dinosaur Momma showed up.

She was much bigger than the kids.

Her teeth were sharper, too.

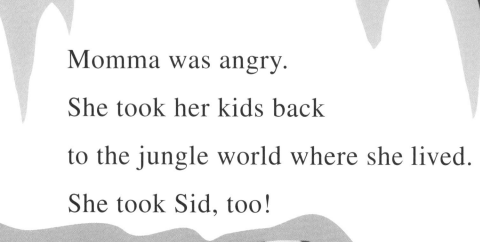

Momma was angry.

She took her kids back

to the jungle world where she lived.

She took Sid, too!

Momma was glad her kids were home,

but she didn't like Sid.

When she growled at Sid,

the kids protected him.

After all, Sid had cared for them!

Momma realized her kids loved Sid.
So instead of trying to eat him,
Momma tried to work with Sid.
But they didn't always agree.

Sid wanted the kids

to eat vegetables.

Momma wanted them to eat meat.

"Grrrr," said Momma.

"That's your answer to everything!"

Sid said.

But sometimes Momma and Sid
were a great team.
At bedtime,
Momma helped Sid into his nest.
She picked him up by his fur.

At first, Sid was scared.

But then he realized

that Momma was just trying to help.

"You're a real softie,

you know that?" he said.

Sid and Momma were getting along,

but Sid felt like

something was missing.

He missed his other friends.

He missed the ice.

Sid knew he didn't belong.

He loved the dinosaurs,

but they were from different places.

It was time for Sid to go home.

A pterodactyl came to get him.

It turned out Sid's friends
had been looking for him!
They missed Sid, too.

Sid loved the dinosaur kids.

But he knew he had to say good-bye.

"You're where you belong," Sid said.

"You'll grow up to be big and tall,

just like Momma."

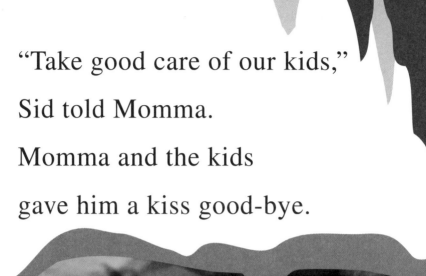

"Take good care of our kids,"
Sid told Momma.
Momma and the kids
gave him a kiss good-bye.

Soon Sid was back in the Ice Age.

His friends were happy to see him.

Sid knew he was where he belonged.